The Lost Humans

Liam Adams

Cover illustration by Liam Adams

The Lost Humans

by Liam Adams

everyoneneedsaliam.com.au

We think this book is mostly suited to young adults, aged from 10-12 onwards, although older adults may enjoy it as much!

This book is sold on the understanding that it is the work of a person with intellectual disability and Autism. All creativity is from the author and the text has been edited by his mother to the best of her ability. However, it is understood that the writing may be different from that expected in a formally published novel.

Liam hopes you enjoy reading his book as much as he enjoyed writing it. He would love to hear your feedback; if you wish to contact him his email address is ltahm@icloud.com

ISBN: 978-0-6455970-2-8
January 2023

Table of Contents

1. Future man in the Laundry Room

After their world was saved and reality corrected, planet Earth wasn't the same old little blue planet it had always been. No hollows or aliens caused any more destruction since a librarian and a company of friends saved reality and corrected the errors.

However, Earth did change so much through the centuries; it was no longer habitable due to many causes including its climate. Humanity started to head off to the stars and carve its own path across the galaxy. They soon found aliens who showed them around the place.

Speeding forward a hundred years:

A nineteen-year-old student called Ryan lived on a space station. He rented his own quarters as he didn't have his own home quite yet. Ryan was transferred to the 'Nautel Galaxy Department' to try to find a life for himself on the station. In the Department, staff gave

Ryan a chance to study the galaxy if he wanted to stay or even work on the station.

Ryan was catching up with a few of his friends on the station today and ordered some takeaway food to take back to his quarters. He and his friends were humans, so they just had normal human food. There was a reason Ryan stayed on the station; he got along very well with his friends on the station and they always had his back.

"So, do you know what you're going to do?" Ryan's friend Kon asked him. Kon had straight black pointy hair that was drowning down on his face, but he said he could see just fine through it.

"Not yet," Ryan told him grimly, "I have been busy doing stuff like studying in my free time and organising the place".

"Have you ever explored the galaxy?" asked Bill, who had long blond hair.

"No, but I've heard Erex is quite warm around this time of the year." Ryan remembered. Ryan was very close with his mates, but he did have other stuff on his mind. "I've heard that there's this booklet".

"Uh-huh" said both Bill and Kon as they nodded their heads.

"I thought you might know of it as well" Ryan commented. "it says I have to learn a lot of things about the station. How to work, how to clean, how even to stay away from the air compressor".

"Please," said Kon, "you know a number of deaths came from that…".

"I know, I know. You don't have to tell me the details".

"Well, the galaxy is a big place, and everything nowadays has all got to do with the galaxy." said Bill who understood quite well about these sorts of things.

"Yeah, but I don't know guys" Ryan told them, "You think travelling across the galaxy is a good idea? Besides, no one ever goes travelling these days".

"That was then and this is now." Bill nodded, which Ryan thought was a good sign. "Things have been rather quiet here. You need to go out there, and experience what none of us ever do".

"Then why do you guys stay here?" Ryan asked.

"Well…why not?" Bill returned.

And then Ryan decided to take his leave.

"Man," said Kon, "I hope we catch up at some point; we don't want any rats coming when you're gone".

"What do you mean?" Ryan asked since he hadn't seen any rats on the station for a while.

"They're all over the place," Kon replied, "They are hideous things; some people here have to keep an eye on them".

Ryan nodded and took off with his takeaway food as he waved his pals goodbye.

****

Ryan returned home to his own quarters. It was a small room, and the light was dim as the whole place grew dark. It was designed to be dim for strange reasons, but Ryan could see easily as the pale light from the ceiling and the lamp near the couch helped him.

He put his takeaway fish and chips on his small coffee table. He sat on the couch as he put on some tv.

Ryan felt so relaxed until he heard a bang in the laundry room. Ryan turned his head and narrowed his eyes, as he had no idea what had happened. He knew he didn't hear things; nothing would have made a big thump that would alert him like that.

He had few choices going through his head; five massive choices he may or may not play. It could be those rats his friends mentioned, but as he thought about it, it sounded louder than a rat could cause.

He got up and walked over to the laundry slowly. The laundry room was a few feet from the couch so Ryan could walk there without any sweat.

The laundry was quite like any normal laundry but a bit more crowded. It had lots of piles of towels he forgot to put away, three laundry machines against a wall, and baskets of clothes. It wasn't the cleanest either; it was like the dustiest laundry on the station. It made Ryan think he should put his laundry on Pexsta Nine: another Space Station that was much nicer than here and had a separate room where anyone could put their laundry to get clean.

As Ryan entered, he saw a man in a red robe looking as though he might have caused the room to become dusty. Ryan could even think this man came with the room, but he hadn't been notified.

"Who are you?" Ryan said to the stranger, "why are you in my laundry?"

"Oh," said the stranger not trying to disturb anything. "I was finding a way in. You don't know where I could find Jack and Vicky, do you?"

Ryan recognised those names. Vicky was a friend of his grandfather Jack; he went out with her for a while long ago. Ryan had no idea who or what this guy was, but saw he had some knowledge about his grandfather.

"Sorry," said Ryan disappointed, "I can't".

"Why not?" the man asked.

"Because Jack was my grandfather," replied Ryan, "I'm his grandson".

The man looked a bit surprised as he stood there, "Wh…?" he replied speechless, "what, what do you mean grandson…boy? kid? whatever you are".

"Who are you?" Ryan asked him curiously; it wasn't quite a demand but was something he was going to think about.

"Oh, it's a bit complicated," said the man mysteriously. "May I come in?"

"You're in my laundry," said the boy. "Why didn't you enter from the front door?"

The stranger walked by him and looked over the room, "I came in the, uh, window".

"But we're on a space station," Ryan told him. "And there's a wall. How can you get through my laundry?!"

"By unexpected explanations" the stranger replied. The stranger known as Floyd looked around the room and observed how different it looked. "I must have travelled through many more generations than I expected." he said, mad at himself.

"Sorry?" Ryan asked as he didn't understand. "Uhh…could you explain everything you told me or can I leave my quarter while you think about it?"

Who was this person? Why is he wearing such daggy clothing and appear not to have any clue about his whereabouts? Most important, WHERE DID HE COME FROM?!?!

The stranger looked back at Ryan, "I thought there was no better way to make an appearance". He sat on the couch comfortably, "Me and your grandfather go way back, and I mean, WAY BACK".

"Way back?" Ryan said, as he thought this guy might be nuts. He saw how young he was, and Ryan had no idea how he knew his grandfather, but not GENERATIONS! "But how did you even meet him back then? You look so young? Are you immortal?"

"Kid," said the stranger, who was giving him some weird serious look, "there are things in the multiverse that kick out the rules of understanding, like Bananas and Cows: they don't make sense to us, but probably they make sense elsewhere".

Then the stranger saw the takeaway food, "You don't mind if I have your fish and chips?" he picked up the food without Ryan's permission. The man ate the food entirely, as quickly as he could eat, CHOM! CHOM! CHOM! He was eating like he hadn't had any food in a hundred years.

"What's your name?" said Ryan, as he wanted to know the stranger.

The man stopped eating as he tried to answer, "Umm...".

"Ryan", the kid offered, "So, when you say way back....?"

"Well, you could say quite far, but not centuries," said Floyd, speaking nonsense, "It was quite hard to tell how long since I met him".

CHOM! CHOM! CHOM! CHOM! this mysterious man couldn't stop eating. He kept eating as Ryan tried to break down who this guy was and what relationship he had with his grandfather. Ryan had great chemistry with his grandfather, but he hadn't known him too much, not entirely.

****

Floor six was a massive area that had food courts and stores over the place. It was a round shape with stairs on two levels. The place had a shiny floor, and everything was full of colour. The roof had a shiny glass diamond that glimmered on the people below.

On the scene was a cop named Nile who sat alone at the food court table that was in the exact centre of the area. He had brown hair with a ponytail; he wore a dark blue jacket in a futuristic police uniform. Underneath he wore a sizzle shirt and shiny black boots that matched with his pants.

He wasn't the toughest guy on the job; he wanted to be, but he knew he wasn't. He just wanted to get the job done. He had been a cop for three years and was getting a handle on the job. He may not be the best of the best, but he did what he had to on the station.

He wrapped up his burger meal. He wanted to hear about any report that was going on at the station. He was a bit impatient if he didn't get a report every few minutes. It was kinda like a check-up thing for him which he cannot stand.

Then his report alarmed him. He took his small hexagon device out. "All right" he said with relief, "time for some business". The tiny device showed him a hologram of the station on every floor with all security. It had some alien lettering that told him about the report.

"An intruder? Appeared in someone's quarters? With no trace?" he said in confusion, "How could someone get in there? No one could ever get in there without a transporter. Unless he had the mind of some complete lunatic" he took the idea in closer "- could they?"

He thought about it more and more and it drove him to feel a bit stupid. He threw his wrap into the nearest bin and stood up from his table. "Time to get to work" he said as he walked out.

****

As Floyd finished the fish and chips, Ryan sat on a chair beside him impatiently. "I came from a far future, and I helped your grandfather stop a big threat in 2016".

"Ah, yeah" Ryan chuckled, "that never happened".

11

"Oh no, it didn't, no one knew it was happening" the man agreed on Ryan's terms. "Anyway, I wanted to come here to ask him if he could come with me on some radical adventures. But it seems like he is not here." he sat there crossly.

"Why not go back and find him?" Ryan thought there could be no better excuse for this mysterious man to leave.

"I tried, but as I tried to look for him, the person it led me to was…", then at that moment, Floyd had an idea as he looked at Ryan.

Ryan looked at the stranger as if he was offering him a gift. "Nah!" Ryan said, refusing, "I can't. I live here".

"What?" said Floyd shocked, "but think of the taste of adventure! Have you tried any?"

"Yeah," Ryan replied.

"Did it taste good?" Floyd added.

"Look!" Ryan said as he tried to get the guy's attention. "If you want to go and hang out with my grandfather, why can't you go back in time and ask him?"

"It doesn't work like that," the stranger said, "and I think if I did it now, it would get very complicated".

"Then… you're stuck here?" Ryan asked.

"Yes," said Floyd.

"That's why you were in my laundry?"

"That's right", Floyd said as he sat on the floor and Ryan just observed.

Floyd sat with no other options. He was here now; where else was he going to? It was as if he hadn't thought this through, which he did, until he completely listened to his inner self rather than his brains.

"Could you ever imagine trying to rewrite one single moment then change things over, over and over again?" Floyd asked Ryan, which made Ryan feel dumb.

"I haven't tried it", Ryan replied, "but if I did, it would be rather a terrible idea to attempt".

"And that's my point exactly", Floyd said as he noticed the tv. Something was spatting right into his direction, and he wasn't paying any attention. He wasn't sure if his eyes were playing tricks or what.

It was showing a report that was saying humans were disappearing. "What?!" he said as he crawled over to the tv, "what did it say?"

"It said humans are disappearing," said Ryan, who wasn't worried.

"Disappearing?" Floyd said in shock, "No, that cannot be. Humans can't disappear; why are humans disappearing?"

"Because we're going to be extinct," said Ryan. Floyd was far from being a moper but was a bit paranoid. This was not meant to happen, this never happened; but it was. And someone was pulling the strings.

2. In Cells

"Nobody can disappear; this is still the golden age of humanity! The biggest events of all history happen now!" Floyd said with outrage and confusion. He wanted to make an undeniable claim, but what statement could he make? "Not even the most common race in all the galaxy could just go out with a blink".

"I have nothing to explain it to you," said Ryan still sitting on the couch, "but it just happened one day".

"Just happened one day?!" Floyd looked at Ryan who thought he was making a fool of himself, but he wasn't. That was the bad of it, "Have you ever reported them?!"

Ryan was startled by the question as it made him worry, "All right, let's not get so ahead of ourselves."

"But people are missing!!" Floyd snapped.

"There has been a big percentage of lost humans in the last year. We don't know really what happened to them, but we all know is we barely see any humans nowadays".

"How?!" Floyd pleaded.

But before Ryan could reply, Nile burst open the door and pointed his futuristic blue gun at Floyd, "Hands in the air!" he called out to Floyd.

"Really?" said Floyd as he put both hands right up in the air, "You and your guns?"

"Well, not even the universe could ignore them," Nile said as he walked over to Floyd, "I am arresting you for trespassing".

"Wait," said Ryan, trying to convince the officer.

"I'm sorry kid," said Nile as he took Floyd by the arm, "Station's rules. You know that by now, and you should really keep out of people's business. And study hard on that booklet".

"But…" Floyd asked.

"Zip it!" Nile snapped.

Ryan stood alone because he knew he couldn't interfere with any of the station affairs. As the door shut, Nile and Floyd walked together through the hallway.

"You should have listened to what that kid was going to say," Floyd complained.

"Shush," Nile said, who wasn't going to take it from a man in a dressing down.

****

Floyd was put in an empty confession cell with hologram walls around him, as Nile was going to integrate him. Nile stood there very serious with his arms crossed.

"OK, here's what's going to happen", Nile started, "you're going to tell me everything you know, all right?"

"You have a nice cell I'll say," Floyd said being distracted, "I say, with few more upgrades, you could really give a light show in here".

Nile wasn't sure if this guy was acting a fool or was just a fool. "All right, what were you doing at the apartment at eleven?"

Floyd looked puzzled as he wondered around the place, "I had some way of getting through places. Well, by some mistakes on the way".

Floyd was thinking about the missing humans in the last hour, and he thought he might break this through to the cop as well, "Do you know that humanity is dying?! And that is not meant to be possible! Whatever is happening to them, and I have no idea what, somebody or something is causing it!"

"Hey, I'm asking the questions," Nile said trying to avoid that matter.

"But you don't think it a bit suspicious?" Floyd asked the officer, listening carefully. "You may think I'm a complete lunatic sneaking his way on the station, but you have to get the authorities onto this! Lives are at stake!"

Nile raised his eyes to Floyd. It seemed he had so little care about his program that he didn't pay any attention. "I'm the authority around here. And if you don't go through by my rules, you'll be in lots of trouble".

"But I'm trying to prevent it from happening," Floyd told the officer.

"And I'm asking the questions! So, who's in a cell and who's isn't?" Floyd was still looking around the place; he couldn't stop himself. "Hey!" Nile spoke up, "you want me to put you somewhere else that isn't so comfortable?"

****

Ryan was sitting at a table with his friends Bill and Kon on floor five, where Floyd was held. After hearing what Ryan heard from Floyd yesterday, he knew his grandfather had been in strange circumstances. Now Ryan couldn't even take his eyes off the police station in the area.

"You were robbed?" Bill asked Ryan.

"No, I wasn't robbed," said Ryan, annoyed for some reason.

"He tried to steal your TV; I can spot any burglar trying to get their hands on that misfiling thing" Kon added.

"Well, he was going for your money, I can tell" Bill added.

"At least you don't have to worry about him," said Kon.

"But he knew my grandfather," Ryan said. He had a weird connection to this stranger that no living being would have. "He knew so much, and spoke like he didn't know anything else, but only important things".

Kon and Bill looked at Ryan worrying, "Are you sure you're OK from yesterday?" Kon asked, "He didn't just mind control you or what?"

"Of course, he didn't" Ryan replied, "Have you ever had some strange family member whom you could feel was there since the very beginning?"

"Beginning of what?" both Bill and Kon asked together.

"Don't know; he was there for centuries".

It was really hard for Ryan to tell; this stranger entered at a very weird time for Ryan, just as he was trying to get his foot around the station. But he had this trigger that alerted him to recognize the stranger.

"Yep, he is definitely mind-controlled," Kon thought.

"It's always when you see it through their eyes", Bill commented, "they kinda turn yellow".

"How you know?" Kon asked curiously.

"Dah, the booklet?!"

Ryan couldn't tell what was wrong with himself. He knew something felt very strange about that stranger, like he knew him from a big history book that got thrown off a boat; or like one of his family members just preferred that this guy was never part of that book.

$$************************$$

In the last forty-seven and five quarters of an hour, Floyd told Nile as much as he could. But sometimes Floyd gave Nile some things that didn't make sense or just weren't part of the question Nile asked him about.

"But all this doesn't apply to what I said," Nile told Floyd impatiently.

"I know" Floyd tried to agree as well. Floyd really didn't care about being trapped in a small room with somebody bothering him with pointless questions that didn't really matter. Floyd really didn't like this sort of thing; he had so many better things to do.

"But you talk about all these things that didn't happen, but again, you read it at a bookstore?" Nile asked.

"Yeah, I've heard it was a top-of-the-class kind", Floyd spoke the truth. "There's this nice freshness within it, and a nice store owner; she's the kindest sort of lady you would ever love to meet".

Nile had quite enough from this man. He was driving him crazy. Nile shook his head and went closer to the forcefield bar, "I'm going to ask you about what happened back at the quarter, and you're going to tell me the truth".

"I already have" Floyd was trying to be reasonable. Then Nile walked off as Floyd stood there with no comment, "What are you doing?"

"See you at court when the PCF comes and gets you." Nile closed the door behind him, and the lights went off beside the one in Floyd's cell. Floyd wasn't too sure if this cop did mean to leave him in the cell or was just going to give him a free Court Lunch.

****

Ryan went over to get his dinner takeaway - he bought smoking hot, fried chips - which wasn't the only time he had chips in less than two days. He was in a massive line-up with many customers.

He noticed that all of them were different species, and none of them were human, which surprised Ryan more. He could recall only thirty humans on the entire station, including himself, his friends, Nile and Floyd.

But where did they all go? Ryan wondered. He wasn't too sure about the full story. It drove him into a bit of a mystery that he couldn't figure out.

"Here you go bud!" said the yellow octopus which gave Ryan his chips.

As Ryan walked back to his quarters, he had much more of a deep thought. Ryan went to his quarters alone; he was trying to get back to his normal routine and his normal life, but he really wanted to see Floyd that night. He just met him, and he had no idea who he was, but he just needed to see him. Ryan had so many questions he wanted to ask him about: What was he? Who was he? Could he even play a Baby Grand Pino? His head was spinning with many, many things but nothing was normal.

He headed toward floor five again and arrived at the entrance of the prison. Nile was standing there as he watched the area around him. Ryan wasn't sure if he wanted to get his foot into any mess or what, but he chose to do the worse, "Hey, you remember me?" he asked the officer.

Nile gave a careless stare where he could identify anyone on the station without listing them on the pinkish report. "Yeah" he replied, as if he thought he forgot about everyone on the station, "don't worry about him, he'll get what he deserves".

"Oh, exactly; I just wanted to speak to him face to face".

Nile put his head down as he knew to not get into anyone's business, including his own. "I would stay out of this one if I were you" he warned Ryan, "He has no clearance on the station, and he hasn't had a clue on how he got in here".

"Well, that's what I was going to say anyway", Ryan explained, "He sent a distress call as he was going to crash miles away, and I hurried to teleport him into my quarter".

Nile narrowed his eyebrows as he thought he should put Ryan in the cell with Floyd, but he shook his head. "But, if you transported him to your quarter, you must have bypassed all of our security systems for beaming on board, traced where he was in space, hacked all of our codes and dialled where you were and placed him into your quarter".

"Well, I must be very clever," Ryan reasoned, as he tried to show off to the officer. But there was a little tension that he was lying. Ryan was a bad liar; he wasn't even good at it; it was awful, just awful!

Nile looked away and looked back, as he wasn't sure what to do. "This Kid is worse at lying than I am," he thought through his brain. Then he walked back inside the prison, "You'll watch out next time" he said as he invited Ryan inside.

3. Blasting off to the Stars

Nile took Ryan through the police office. There were desks around the room and the room itself was in a hexagon shape. The corners had hallways, mostly leading to the prisoners' cells. But Nile was leading Ryan toward the interrogation room, where the door slid open.

On the other side of the room, Floyd was still inside the forcefield bar, surprised to see Ryan. Ryan looked at Nile as he stood there, watching Ryan and Floyd at the same time.

"What? You think I would leave you here with him?" Nile asked Ryan, as he wasn't going to leave him alone with a stranger.

"I wish you had chairs or something" Floyd argued, "my legs have been aching for these last couple of days".

Ryan looked at Floyd who was interested in why he was here.

"So, what brings you by, hmm?" Floyd asked curiously.

"You mentioned something about my grandfather. How did you really meet him?" Ryan tried to answer him, but Floyd just stood there with nothing on his mind.

"OK", Floyd started, "it was only a one-time thing, so I didn't really know him that well; it was only a drop-in-and-go thing".

Ryan shrunk with disappointment. All of this was pointless, he thought. Even if Floyd was lying, he knew something that Ryan didn't.

"But why are you here where he isn't; why were you led to me?"

"No clue. Probably you were his closest bloodline, so it might have led me to you instead".

Floyd looked at Nile carefully and wished the cop would leave them alone for one second, but that would be very unlikely. Floyd then looked at Ryan closely.

"But right now, I want to know everything you know about what happened to the lost humans." Floyd said to Ryan in a quiet voice so that Nile couldn't hear. "It is very important to me if something bad has happened to them".

Ryan looked back at Nile who was still watching them. He looked back at Floyd who asked "Which part of space did they go to?"

Ryan was trying to remember. "What I have heard, a lot of people headed to Talen Space - why?"

Floyd was trying to put all the pieces together as he tried to imagine all the facts he knew already. He counted his fingers as he tried to do math in his head, while recalling useful information. It seemed bits of that was working and the rest was useless.

"If they all went to Talen Space, it may be that something is lurking," Floyd said, as if it could be a real option, "pulling them somewhere".

"Wait", Ryan said a bit louder, "You think there's someone that is kidnaping humans?"

"Maybe," Floyd thought, "but what if it wasn't someone, but something?"

Then an alarm sounded at the station, lights flashed red, and Floyd's bars disappeared. Ryan and

Floyd were blanked and saw Nile opening the door out
of the police area.

"We have to go!" Nile demanded.

"WHAT?!?!" Floyd and Ryan said together,
"JINX!!!"

Nile left them with Floyd halfway out of the cell.

"Wait" Ryan said to him, "I never caught your
name?"

"Floyd," said the stranger finally.

Then both Floyd and Ryan ran after Nile.

****

The station was alarmed and everyone panicked
and wondered what was going on. Floyd, Nile and Ryan
ran through the station, avoiding the people around
them.

Shortly after they arrived at a door; it said
'VEHICLE PORTING AREA', which meant it was
where the vehicles were parked. Nile pulled the handle

of the door to open it so they could get inside the stairs leading them deep down.

They later arrived at the vehicle area where they walked on a platform that was hovering in a space that was cast by a small force field. The only reason they could breathe was that there was also a small force field for them surrounding the station.

Vehicles were parked in a line, all different and well-designed. Nile pointed out "There!" at his vehicle. It was a purple looking 90s car of some sort, with no wheels but hovers. It had no windows but a big fresh air force field around it.

They jumped into Nile's car, Floyd flipping into the back with Ryan. With so many things were happening so fast at once, Floyd just had to ask, "Why are you helping us?"

"Because I believe you," Nile told him; that was as far he would go. Believe what?

But Floyd couldn't buy it. "But you're helping us; why does what I said to make you believe me?"

Then they could hear sounds nearby. Nile looked up as the flashlights of the PCF drones were coming -

they were golden and labelled the PCF. They also had a red and blue flashlight on the top of their heads, and they each had a white square wide eye.

Nile's vehicle took off and sped through space. The passengers tried to hold on but Floyd fell over in the back seat. "Seat belts!!" Nile called out.

When they were many kilometres away from the space station, Ryan looked back and noticed how far away he was going, but that was the least of his troubles.

"INCOMING!!!" he called as he ducked his head.

The drones were fast on their tail as lasers blasted above them. Nile caught their attention as he dodged one way then another. It made Floyd uneasy about Nile's driving skills that he was pulling off.

"Can you stop that?" Floyd tried to ask Nile nicely. But that wasn't going to help.

The drones took a clear shot at the back of Nile's vehicle as Floyd and Ryan ducked under cover.

Floyd was mad at them as he looked at them and called, "Leave me alone!" in anger.

As they flew lighting fast in this chase, Nile took a few turns a couple of times to get the drones off their tails. Floyd fell on the floor many times as Nile kept on turning.

They were entering into deeper space where they hardly could see the space station, but the drones were still with them.

"How many times are you going to do this?" Ryan asked the cop while Floyd couldn't take a breath.

"Because these guys don't give up" Nile said as he kept trying to lose them.

Floyd returned to his spot as they kept a good distance from the drones.

"What is this all about, really?!" Floyd asked the cop. "There was some sort of reason you wanted us out of the station?! Why do you believe me?!"

"Yes, yes I did!" said Nile as he looked at Floyd directly, "because I escaped from Talen Space. Barely alive. And I don't get why you would ever want to get involved with this".

"That's why you risked your career!" Ryan called out.

"Yeah, maybe I'll get some years off my work, but I thought if you wanted to help out, why not…".

At that moment, the drones flew directly over Nile's vehicle and took a good shot as it exploded!

The drones hovered to check that there was no evidence of any life signs as pieces of the vehicle floated in space. They later headed back to the station as there was nothing left of Floyd and his new friends. Their mission had already failed before it ever began.

4. Dying in Space

It was dark in space as the Nile's vehicle shattered, its engines destroyed, and with the coldness that nobody could save them. The passengers only had a few minutes of air left. They were sitting on their seats with their eyes badly open; they could do nothing but sit there.

"SIXTEEN PERCENT OF OXYGEN LEFT," said the vehicle's computer, still active, "YOU HAVE ONLY FIVE MINUTES OF AIR LEFT".

Great, they all thought. They think things couldn't get any badder than getting stuck out in the vacuum of space where you could hardly breathe. I mean, how much of a bummer is that?

Everyone wanted to wake up, wake the others by slapping at their faces and figure out what to do next, but that wasn't possible in this circumstance. With the condition they were all in, they could not move as their bones froze mid-movement.

Floyd was the one who wanted to wake up the most. He briefly saw a massive ship coming by; he couldn't tell what it looked like or what its features were, even though that would fascinate him even at a time like this. Floyd passed out like the others, not knowing whether help did arrive or not. It was too late.

✱✱✱✱✱✱✱✱✱✱✱✱✱✱✱✱✱✱✱✱✱✱✱

Floyd was waking up; his head was dizzying around; he could also hear music that he knew wasn't part of his accident. Funky music, in fact. Funky Music? Is that what everyone would've heard when they returned from a big and horrible coma?

He looked up when he saw a floor made entirely of bamboo, as he could also see through it. He saw colours flashing above the floor. They flashed like those flashy lights at parties. He mostly saw a lot of green and purple around the place.

Floyd could see people dancing on different floors, through the bamboo. There was bamboo everywhere, like it was sticking to the place.

The place was so huge that Floyd couldn't tell what was at the bottom or at different sides of the area. This was some weird, strange place.

He knew he could see almost everything, but he couldn't tell where he was; he didn't know what had happened to him. It still made Floyd's head dizzy.

He looked around him as he tried to figure out where he was. Floyd had many guesses about what happened to him when he died, but he could tell this was not how people die normally.

Then a guy, or a dude you could say, from above stared down at Floyd and then jumped down to greet him. "Hey, man", he told him, as if it meant 'hello' in some way.

Floyd wasn't sure if he wanted to start greeting himself after some weird blackout. He didn't quite remember yet, "Where…" said Floyd as he stood up but banged his head on a bamboo pole, "where am I?"

The man helped Floyd walk. He had curly black hair, and his face needed a shave. He had a purple sleeveless jacket and it seemed he was part of whatever party group this was.

"I have a few friends of mine", Floyd continued, not in a good condition, "well, not friends. I only knew them a little. One of them is my friend's grandson and a cop that somehow helped me but arrested me then he broke me out".

"Hold on, hold on," said the man, interpreting, "you need to rest first".

Floyd lay down, looking at the guy. What is this? he thought as his brain tried to make sense out of it; who was this guy? He didn't look like the kind of guy who would catch him from the crash. Too many questions, too many questions. Then Floyd said, "But I have to find my friends".

The man looked as if he might well know where they were. He gave him a look as if he knew something – in a good kind of way, Floyd hoped. "I'll take you to your friends after you rest a bit".

"Ok" Floyd didn't argue; he looked up at the place as if he didn't know where he was, "what is this place?"

"The Coucal Plane," said the man.

"The what?" Floyd thought.

"It's the name of the ship," the man explained. It didn't look like any ship could be built like this, Floyd thought. It's too strange, like the people who made the bamboo and hidden parts of the ship's engines and other components. How is it moving? What's controlling it?

"But it can't be", Floyd refused to acknowledge, as he couldn't imagine that. "No ship could make just a place for misfits who think they are from party heaven." he said with a slight chuckle. "What kind of ship is this?"

"A cruise ship," the man told Floyd. Floyd started to get up and the man helped him walk again.

****

They walked further up the ship; it was like a party ship with people all over. When Floyd and party dude walked to the upper level, it looked different. The bamboo straws were dispersing as they walked further up, and the massive party area was in darkness below.

The stairs and the floors were still bamboo, but the weird thing was the walls; the walls were like a blank of darkness that looked like you were looking into the abyss in the far distance.

They walked up the longer and more dangerous stairs where no more than five people could walk simultaneously. It was a large area where crew members came down and about.

The guy kept chatting to Floyd about the ship and all the cool facts and details. Floyd should've felt worn out by his company but was really interested. "We're stranded in space with nowhere else to go".

Floyd still couldn't believe a word coming out of his mouth, "But…have you ever headed to nearby planets? Transports? Space Stations? Brunches?"

"There weren't any nearby," the man replied, "and why bother?"

"What?" Floyd said, confused and wasn't going to skip on that matter, "but there was one nearby; why didn't you trace that? there could be plenty more random people on board if you just go and visit".

"Nah, we have enough as it is." Floyd was thrown by this response. "Besides," continued the dude, "we couldn't enter that part of space", the man explained, "wherever we go, we can't enter any kind of sector space or find a planet in our locators; we're stuck out here".

"And you're cool with that?" Floyd asked a personal question.

"Yeah, we're fine," the dude said cheaply, with no worries in the universe.

Floyd didn't know how this was possible, but he might have a wild guess - Talen Space. Whatever happened to the human race, all led there; good reason why they were all paranoid.

But Floyd wondered, "How long have you been stuck out here?"

"Oh, well," said the man, as he tried to remember, "Twelve years? Maybe fifteen?"

"What?!" Floyd exclaimed, as he got his consciousness back, "all that time, and you couldn't find anywhere to lay low? You've been all living in this illusion?!"

It was a crazy story, but these people couldn't go anywhere. Their stuff wasn't advanced and didn't have special technology; there must be some kind of backstory behind this that Floyd could put his thought to.

"It all happened when we entered Talen Space," the bloke said, as they arrived at the top floor where the corridor and everything else was bamboo.

Floyd turned and said, "You entered Talen Space? What happened there?"

The dude wished he could remember, but he hardly thought about what happened, "It…it was a dumb story, sorry".

"That's ok," Floyd said as they kept walking, "we were planning on heading to Talen Space, anyway".

"Good luck," the dude said, stuttering, "it will be your death wish, man".

They walked through the long corridor. There were rooms with no doors, some rooms for the crew, others for the passengers, but there was currently a medical room nearby.

Floyd saw the room on their left.

"Hey". Floyd asked his new friend, "are we meant to be heading over there?"

"Oh no," said the man as they walked to another room on the right, "this is where your friends are".

They were about to enter the room, which Floyd found out later was the Crew's Medical 'Peridots' room. They turned around as they had taken the wrong turn.

"It's the next one ahead," the guy said.

They later arrived at the right room where a few people were sick and hurt. Beds with curtains over them lined the room as Floyd and the other guy walked further in. Floyd saw Ryan and Nile near a bed. Ryan spotted Floyd and called out, "Floyd!"

Floyd ran up to him as he was so glad they were all alive and weren't suffocated in outer space. Nile was sitting down on the bed, healing from his injuries in space.

"How are you?" Floyd asked Ryan as he couldn't believe his eyes. How was there some connection between them? Who knew, they thought.

"Fine", Ryan replied, "we thought you were dead".

"Couple of shots and dying without oxygen? I don't think so," Floyd thought that might not be how his story ended. Not unless it had him dying sitting in a comfortable chair gazing out on the sunset with rice paddies and eating at least a cake.

"I could end up by a…" he stopped as he saw Nile gave him a worrying stare; Floyd thought he had better not say it.

He walked up to Nile and stood awkwardly, "Sooooo...you been to Talen Space, I can see?"

****

Nile told Floyd and Ryan all he knew about Talen Space; he escaped a few years ago when he was younger. He knew much of what was in there and who was causing all this.

"They say it is the trap of the humans," Nile unravelled his story, "no one ever leaves Talen Space; when you enter it, you'll never get out, ever!"

"But these people left it," Ryan said, "why do you think nobody could escape?"

"Because it rarely happens," Nile said, as he knew it was almost impossible.

"It is the tragedy of the human race; you will never get out. There's no other way around it".

Floyd didn't know precisely what was causing it, but he knew that something was lurking in Talen Space; he knelt forward.

"Nile," he told him, "whatever is in there, whatever has happened to the human race, I must do something about it".

"You?" Ryan asked Floyd, as if he thought it was a joke, "you're going to stop what's inside, in your robe?"

Sure, stopping a group of nut-head lizard aliens causing mass destruction in the timeline is one thing. But trying to save humanity is another challenge altogether.

"Me?" Floyd told Ryan, "I'm not going alone; you're coming with me, the both of you".

"Me?" said Ryan as if that was a stupid offer, "why me?"

"Your grandfather said he owed me, so you're coming with me, kid," Floyd told him. Then he looked at Nile sitting down in silence, "What about you, cop?"

"I, uh," he said, as he wasn't sure about coming along, "are you sure about this?"

"I'm not sure about anything," Floyd stated out loud, thinking he may be making the biggest mistake in his life, "but look how far it got me".

"We got shot at," Nile reminded him as he thought Floyd would be the wrong guy for the job, "and as we are all here, can you really believe we can trust you? – again?"

"The other guy did," Floyd said.

"What guy?" Ryan asked curiously.

"You, young one," Floyd said as it was Ryan's secret nickname; he gave him a soft slap on the head for good luck. "So, coming or not?"

Nile had some troubling times in Talen Space; he knew the stories about what was in Talen Space. But one thing was he knew he was no coward.

He got up heroically, "What's our move?"

There, the trio stood as they were about to make a bracing journey to save humankind; they felt so heroic in some way. They haven't done anything, except run away, get shot down and find each other again. But that all changed here.

Floyd planned his first move. "What we should do first is that you should put your gun away", he told Nile, "I think we can use other stuff than that".

Nile pulled out his gun, placed it in a draw next to him and closed it inside.

5.   A Spy in the Camp

After Floyd's first action of the plan, the next step was getting Nile to change his clothes. It was shouting trouble, and it felt a bit uncomfortable when around people. It was also torn when it was in space; people said that's how he looked when they found him. Ryan's clothes were also torn, so he and Nile went to the clothing area.

There were free clothes for anyone; not only were they very hippy, but they also had some regular clothes.

Floyd made his way to an excellent food court area where they were selling lovely cupcakes and other stuff. Floyd thought the cupcakes were the only thing he could eat; everything else was full of sparkles and tasted weird.

Nile was trying on some tights that were a bit strict of his zone; Ryan was wearing some big jeans and jumpers that wouldn't fit so he had to keep trying other stuff. He thought his regular clothes would work, but he did admit to Floyd that they were in no condition.

Ryan found the right clothes to work for him; he wore a standard T-shirt and some runners. Nile was still trying to get his tights together. "How are you going?" Ryan asked the cop.

He could hear him fiddling as he was having a bit of trouble. Facing bad guys was not a problem; getting stupid tights on? That was a problem. "They Won't Fit!" he snapped; he never had these problems at the station, probably because the shops would identify what would fit who.

Nile was fighting with himself, "I don't get why your friend doesn't need changing!"

"He never asked," Ryan replied, as he knew Floyd wasn't going to get rid of that Robe in his entire life. "However, he is not my friend".

"But why do you defend him?" Nile asked, as he didn't think it made any sense.

Ryan had a weird connection with Floyd since he went all talkative; there was something about him, but he couldn't make out what. Maybe it was all true what

Floyd said. "I don't know; he has something that really understands me".

"Like How?"

"Like I know him". It was weird; he had this feeling for Floyd whenever he met him. It was like if a couple of eggs see each other, they'll crash into each other and SLAPT!!

Ryan couldn't tell; he may never tell. Then came Nile; he wore a button-up shirt with a leather jacket. The tights indeed fit him infernally. "Come on," he said to Ryan, "let's go find your friend".

****

Ryan and Nile went into some sort of room with people wandering around. The great thing about these places was that the flashy lights had departed, and standard light beamed down into the entire room.

Bad news: Floyd was not to be seen. He must have gone off and found other food to test while spitting out what did not work for him. Nile was standing impatient as he tried to look out for him, "Gosh", he said to himself. He looked back at Ryan, who felt like a regular Teen entering a weird world. Nile kneeled down and kept a straight face, "Look, I'm going to find Floyd". Ryan didn't refuse the police officer as Nile wandered off.

Nile had no clue where the misfit went; he could be anywhere. Every lead he had always led him to a dead wall.

Without searching less than halfway through the place, Nile came face-to-face with a man in a hood. He wore a grey raincoat. His face looked old and suspicious, and his eyes glimmered with a familiar look that Nile must have seen that face before.

"Hello, Golan," the man said to Nile. Nile's past name was Golan, but he had never used that name since he left Talen Space. Nile was studying the mysterious man's face to remember who he was.

It took him several guesses until he found out who this guy was. He was a spy. He had seen him before, but his memory was foggy; he couldn't remember what, when and how? But he knew he caused trouble. "How nice to bump into you in such a place as this?" he said, very shady and full of evil.

Nile thought at that moment, I should've brought my gun; this guy could do anything, but I could stop him here and now. The problem he had though, was that this man had hidden a small gun-like device in his coat.

"I wouldn't try causing a scene," he said, trying to put that thought into Nile. Nile wasn't pleased. "I know my way right, left, back and forward. There is no way you could escape from my eye".

Nile wanted to slap the weapon out of his hand, but he knew he was well-trained, better than himself. He had been trained for evil and Warsop, their god. But what god? Nile remembered. Who was it?

The man waved his hand for Nile to follow. They walk out of the area near a balcony where the stairs led.

Nile felt the tension of his enemy; he wanted him out of his plans, or mostly, their plan. Whomever Nile and Floyd were facing, they might have targets on their backs without noticing it.

The man still looked at him. When Nile tried to tilt his head, he knew he was still watching him. There was no way out of this, was there? Maybe except for one…

He took a slow turn away from the balcony. He had the feeling this might be at his own risk. The man was about to shoot Nile when Nile quickly kicked him off the balcony, broke the fence that kept the patio safe, and the man fell.

Many people came to see him fall but they weren't sure what they saw. Was it a goat? No, it was a man, in fact. Falling to his death and not expecting what he was in for.

Ryan ran towards Nile as he took notice of the massive accident. "What was that?!" he wondered, "did you see what happened?"

"I don't know", Nile lied, "but I have the feeling this ship is not just a cruise".

Then not so far away, Floyd passed by and spotted them, "Uh, Hello", he said to them happily, "have you both found anything interesting?"

6. Arm Wrestle!

Floyd, Ryan and Nile thought they needed to plan this outrageous mission, and they thought they needed a way to get to Talen Space in some kind of spacecraft.

They only just arrived, and they didn't have any idea if these DJ blokes had any ships docked.

They marched over the cruise ship to see if there were any smaller ships on board. Floyd led his pals through corridors and steep stairs, tracing his steps, he thought.

He hadn't any idea where he was going or where he was leading his friends. They arrived at a wall of straws and, later, another dead end with a wall of straws. They went downwards and upwards as they kept finding another excuse they were lost. His friends thought he might be lost, but he denied it.

As someone who knew about almost everything that happened in history, he may as well know where he was going.

They were walking down the steep stairs once again and kept coming back and forward.

"Face it"; said Ryan with precision, "you're lost".

"No, I'm not!" Floyd denied it. He looked around the floor trying to think where to go, "I say, we go that way".

"You're just suggesting." Ryan told Floyd as if it was the truth.

"No, I'm not!" Floyd said clearly, and then his friends turned to a different direction.

Floyd looked blank, "Where are you going?"

"The right way," Nile said as they walked down.

****

They were on one of the bottom floors where the place was more like a party with flashing lights everywhere. The space still had its bamboo - you get the picture of the area. The bamboo walls on the right were so intense it seemed like behind it was made of metal.

What the gang could spot as they walked up was a few people surrounding a door, a standard door that did not make sense. The front guy was trying to open it, pretending to use a powerful tool in his hand. He later banged his hands on it as he didn't have any other option left.

"Hey," Ryan called to the guy, "do you guys have a shipping dock on board?"

"So, we could get out of here?" Floyd asked pertly. "Not because I don't like this place, I do. It's just because we really want to get out of here".

The people stared at them, curious, but with one of those 'you're really not going to like this' faces.

"Well, if you found the passport to open this thing," said the man, "we could get inside and assess it. We try to open it, but it blocks us off".

It looked like the code to the place must be good. Technology doesn't look too much in a place like this, but they do have a small amount of technology.

"How could we find the passport?" Ryan asked, as if he wanted to help.

"Well, you have to ask Blok," the guy said.

"Blok?" Nile asked, "Who's he? Your boss?"

"No," the guy responded, "He…is the ship's Tech expert".

"Cool," Floyd said with no worry, "Where is he?"

"Oh, on floor seven at the top side," the guy explained it like it was a bad thing, "but he may not give it to you; he is really concerned about anybody getting those codes".

Floyd laughed, "How could some guy be concerned about a thing like that?"

"Mostly because he is a jerk".

"Well, we'll just pay him a little visit, and we'll see he changes his mind", Floyd replied as if this would be a piece of cake.

****

Floyd, Ryan and Nile went upstairs to floor seven. They wondered who this Blok guy was on the way and if this guy was a big problem. The others said he was. He might be some tough guy that they didn't drag down to the bottom floor only to open the door.

"Maybe this might not be a good idea," said Ryan as they stopped.

"What are you talking about?" Floyd asked as he wasn't sweating at that moment. "We can take those passports off him in no time. It's not like we would steal them off him".

Nile crossed his arms as he looked at Floyd; Floyd gave him a funny smile. "Well, as you have forgotten," Nile spoke up, "getting a passport off somebody may be an offence in the law. But I am helping you, so there's that".

"See?" Floyd told Ryan as he patted his belly, "you have to be more like Nile, Ryan? He knows what action to take when it comes".

They stepped inside the room; it was a medium room with chairs in an empty space and a random couch that was there for some reason. But what made the room really ring was a wrestling ring at the centre.

Floyd and Nile couldn't tell why it was on board, but they knew they had asked and seen enough when it came to this party ship.

Over on the other side of the room, they saw a tough guy a few feet away chatting to some of his engineers at a DJ record player. They were having a meaningful conversation about something.

Floyd and his friends felt bad about interrupting, but they felt like they had been on this ship long enough and should really move on. Floyd stepped forward and coughed for their attention.

The tough guy turned and looked at Floyd. Here Floyd should have felt a bit shaken by the guy rather than relaxed.

"Blok, isn't it?" he asked, "we heard you were giving out the passports. If you give us some, we will be off".

Blok was a big guy; he had a blond-shaven head with ears that could be floppy, or they were just made that way. He had a black sleeveless shirt and big-length eyes that could see deep into your soul.

"Give you passports? Is that so?" Blok said as if he thought these guys were going to annoy him rather than distract him from work. "I don't give out passports anymore; these days, I normally chill and party out".

"Seriously?" said Ryan, who was going to giggle, "Party out?"

"Hey!" Floyd said as he walked up to Blok, "we didn't come this far to be stopped by…by some guy…".

"This guy…" said Blok looking down on Floyd in his shadow, "…may have other plans for Mr strawberries wizard and friends, and we don't want that, do we?"

Floyd had a deep thought, thinking he was reading the mind of Blok. These other plans Blok spoke of might affect their journey. "A matter of fact…".

"Hey," Nile interrupted before Floyd could do anything stupid, "maybe we could make a deal?"

Floyd was still thinking that he was reading the mind of Blok and that he could still beat him. Floyd was the hawk, Blok was the turtle; Floyd had no other roles for his sidekicks, but he knew he could swipe Blok before he could respond.

"A deal?" Blok replied with interest, "I think a deal might be on offer. But I'll give you your passport only if you challenge me to something".

Floyd wasn't sure what Blok might offer, but he had to take whatever would come his way if his plan didn't work. "You name it," Floyd replied, as if he was confident, but he wasn't.

Blok gave Floyd an unconformable smile and determined the challenge. "If you wrestle me in the ring?"

Floyd's face turned upside down with his eyes wide up and eyebrows pointing. Floyd had never wrestled in his entire life; at least never wrestled anybody who was ten times his own size as Blok was. "I can't wrestle!" he called out.

"Well, no wrestle, no passport", Blok said, stating his own rules.

"Wait!" Nile spoke out, "I'll challenge you!"

"You will?" Floyd said, a bit relieved.

"Won't do", Blok refused, "facing a cop isn't a fair challenge". He must have seen Nile in his police uniform from earlier.

"Make it two, me and Floyd versus you," Nile said instead.

"Done", Blok agreed.

"Wait!" Floyd disagreed, "I'm not wrestling".

"What?" Nile said, as if he thought Floyd was making things even worse.

"But I will arm wrestle!!!" Floyd declared.

"Floyd", Ryan whispered to him behind, "you know this is our only way".

"Yes, I do," Floyd said back to Ryan, "but how am I supposed to take down a guy that looks so buff?"

Ryan was thinking of suggestions, "Pretend he isn't so buff".

Floyd imagined that if Blok wasn't a tough guy, he would smash Blok in a basketball match all by himself. Then Floyd turned to Ryan, "Actually, that helped a little bit".

****

Floyd and Nile were in the ring with Blok. They sat down on their stools around a clean white table - two on one. Blok lay both of his arms out as Floyd and Nile each put one of their arms out.

Blok had massive muscles that Floyd didn't want to think about. It would haunt him before the match began, but that only would let Blok win, and Floyd wasn't going to let that happen.

The referee was some kind of blue lime squid alien with a tentacle moustache; he also had lots of squid-like feet and was wearing a regular referee shirt. He stood in the centre of them, "OK, ready…".

"I'm not ready", Floyd whispered to himself.

"Get set…"

"Not sure this was a good idea".

"GO!"

Floyd's arm was almost touching the table when they started; Nile was wrestling Blok's other arm on the other side.

Floyd was right; he was not ready for this. But he knew he couldn't give up now, he tried slowly to pull his arm up, but Blok was trying to push it down as he struggled with Nile.

Nile and Blok's arms struggled to battle each other on which titan would fall and which one would rush to the burrito store.

As Nile pulled down Blok's arm inches towards the table, Blok pulled it back to the centre.

Floyd didn't go anywhere better; he struggled a lot with one massive hand he could hardly move. Floyd's hand came with a plan to slowly pull Blok's arm a bit higher as much as he could, and then Floyd gained an upper hand to win this pitiful competition.

As Nile lay his hand at the centre with Blok, Blok had no idea what move Nile was planning next. He could flaw him off and beat him, easy as that. Blok tried to push Nile's hand down.

But what Blok didn't realize was that Nile wanted him to do that. He twisted his hand and as his hand switched, Blok's arm got close to the table; but Blok refused to lose.

Floyd was trying to will himself to win. He wanted to win. He pulled much higher and higher until he reached Blok's hand at the centre. He had a better advantage, and then he realized that Nile was helping him. Blok couldn't believe his eyes; he was losing. Blok faced the fact that he couldn't win; Nile had his fun.

Nile and Floyd touched Blok's arms on the table simultaneously. Blok fell backwards from his stool as Floyd stood up and put both hands in the air with a fist as he won.

"I did it", he said to himself, surprised, "I DID IT!!!".

Blok looked up in disappointment. He had given them his word and wanted to respect their victory. "You'll have it," he said, disappointed, as he threw the passport on the table.

Without noticing the passport, Floyd celebrated so hard that he hadn't a care in the universe.

****

Much later, as the door to the dock was opened by the passport, Floyd, Ryan, and Nile tried to get a ship that would take them out of this place. The dock was big, blue and, for the first time, wasn't made from bamboo. It felt like the docking for the ships was the same size as the party ship itself.

They found a nice-looking ship called the Edwin; a big, sleek silver ship made with nice scrap. There was a wide black sleek window at the top and other black windows on the other side of the ship with a wonky line that led towards the centre.

They were sitting in the piloting room with Nile piloting. Floyd felt left out because Nile thought Floyd would just make things worse. But there was a big clear window they could see through and two long seat rows.

Floyd sat next to Nile as he was looking at the beautiful controls in front of him.

"Look at that" Floyd said as he knelt forward.

Nile pushed Floyd back and took up the ship's wheel.

"No"; Nile told him. "Weren't you supposed to be with Ryan so that you won't touch anything?"

Floyd wished he didn't listen to a word Nile said to him but looked at Ryan behind him snoring.

Then Floyd said unpleasantly, "Yes".

Nile smiled as the Edwin took off and drawled outwards leaving the Coucal Plane. And so they marked their way into Talen Space, the last place you ever wanted to go in the galaxy.

7. Finding Old Friends

On the way through the massive galaxy, Nile knew how to control the ship as they were again in the plane of space. Stars shone across thousands of miles and light glimmered at them as they passed by.

Floyd and Ryan returned to the piloting room after wandering through the ship. Ryan had never been on a spaceship like this; well, not one that he could explore like a nice stylish ship with incredible halls.

"So, Talen Space?" Floyd asked Nile.

Nile pressed a few buttons as he set his course, "We have to go somewhere first".

"But there are people, our people, stranded out there," Ryan reminded him. Why would they go somewhere else first rather than head to their destination? Whatever it was, it must be significant.

Nile had a foggy past that both Ryan and Floyd couldn't read; he was more mysterious than they could work out. Every time they moved to know the guy, he has some weird excuse for something. Deep down, Nile knew he had to save those people, no matter what. "We will; it's about the ones that helped me got out of there", he said with concern. "They made a base for themselves along here".

"Allies!" called Floyd by himself as Nile and Ryan turned their heads, nodding, "I like it! I've never been part of a rouge group".

"You should," Nile thought that was the kind of thing Floyd might like. Floyd would've liked anything that came out of his own mouth.

****

A few miles before heading into Talen Space, they stopped at a station that looked pretty crammed and not something you would always like to see. It was bendy and had a large sized disc on the top. There were windows all around that showed different colours popping out. They could easily hear music inside, but

Nile and the others planned not to stay long. Not only that, but Floyd also smelt something quite stale. It wasn't the kind of place that would have a friendly welcome sign; more like "We Better Get Going! SO…Get Lost or else!"

They landed their ship at the shipping dock; there were a few men around that were either cleaning, putting away some heavy cargo into their silver ships, or just relaxing and playing their guitars.

Behind the next big shield door lay a long stair leading upwards. They arrived at a large area with a few men playing cards. There was another table where a few guys were doing nothing. But one of them had the radio on; that's where the music came from.

Floyd and the others passed over them as they weren't doing much. "Don't encourage them", Nile warned Floyd, "you'll get into trouble".

"Ah, good", said Floyd as he winked at them. It was a weird gesture; Nile felt Floyd meant to cause trouble, that Floyd was no fighter, and that even if he didn't get into a fight, Ryan would hold him down just in case.

"No, not my trouble, they're trouble," Nile explained as he warned him clearly. There was one man who waved to Floyd, and to whom Floyd gave a more nervous wave back.

"I am not a fan of this place", Floyd replied, "why are we here?"

"An old friend," Nile told him. "Well, not exactly a friend; we just heard stories about him; he goes by the name of the Legendry Ga 'telly".

"Ga 'telly?" Floyd said to himself as he thought it sounded cool.

"Who is he?" Ryan asked Nile, who wished to be part of their conversion because he felt left out.

Nile looked back at Ryan, "He is the Revolutionary leader; if we could talk to Gemmill, he'll talk".

"Who's Gemmill?" Ryan asked, thinking what's with all these secrets? What is Nile really hiding?

"Gemmill - she is the Revolutionary Commander in Talen Space", Nile explained as there was more to share, "and she is also Ga 'telly's wife".

"BOMBSHELL!!!!" Floyd called out quietly.

"NO WAY!!!!" Ryan thought as things started to unravel quickly.

"If Ga 'telly tells us information about what's inside Talen Space and talks to Gemmill, they might be some help to us".

Hope was the only word that flowed through Ryan and Floyd's heads. Will they even be likely to help or not? Maybe not?

****

They walked up a few more pairs of stairs until they entered an abandoned room dotted with odd sorts of stuff. It was a kind of place where it felt like somebody lost a random spare room that they never imagined ever existed but disappeared.

Light bulbs dangled from above and torn and burnt books tumbled on the other side of the room. Near a cosy chair were small computers with screens of the station that showed almost everywhere. It had the docking bay where they could see the Edwin; there were the men playing cards, and they could easily see one guy's cards cheating.

The room was very messy, and Ga 'telly wasn't there.

"Where is this Ga 'telly?" Floyd asked as he wandered over the room.

Floyd was distracted by the cameras and buttons. Ryan walked over to a man sleeping in his bed next to the books. He had white hair and was badly shaved; he was wearing torn clothes that weren't clean either.

Ryan might feel bad if he disturbed the gentleman or if he told the other two in the room about it. However, just then Floyd pressed a button that alarmed the gentleman to jump out of his bed, freaking out when he saw Ryan up to his face. He dropped down on the floor.

"What have I told you not to touch anything!" Nile called out to Floyd, who turned around and smiled at the officer. To all that happened on this journey, Floyd really didn't like Nile's rules; yes, he put guns away, but that was Floyd's idea, and that was good.

Ga 'telly was getting up to his table to greet his guests. "Hello there!" he said very lightly, "I've heard you came to join the Revolutionary!"

Floyd, Nile and Ryan looked at each other, not understanding whether this was the guy, but strangely it was. Nile knew this was the guy, so the other two accepted it. Then they looked back at Ga 'telly.

"We actually didn't", Ryan told him, refusing the offer oddly.

"Oh", said Ga 'telly, who felt odd too, "then what can I do for you?"

The group were a bit curious about the guy; how strangely he spoke to them, like he was making a riddle that you could easily guess by the letter he spelt from the last letter of the word he said. And he always kept his eyes wide.

Nile went closer to the man, "I don't know what your memory is like now, but do you remember me?" Nile asked Ga 'telly, "I was part of your escape squad".

"Oh yes!" he said as if he could remember, but he didn't really; he thought better not to bring it up, "The finest man I could have counted on!"

Nile had a bad thought of what he was about to ask, but this was the kind of question he was prepared for, "We need some guidance into Talen Space".

Ga 'telly flew his arms wildly as if he thought Nile gave him a heart attack for some reason.

"Ooooooh, you should be warned before entering in such a place", he said with his voice vanishing into a quite ghostly voice. "There are men on the surface, they keep an eye on everyone down there and later take them to the evil one".

"What are they?" Ryan asked, scared, although he tried not to be.

Ga 'telly's eyes turned over the place as it went into their eyes again.

"They are called the Shatter Clouds," he said in the most scared way possible. "You must watch each other; they will catch you right away, and they won't rest".

"That's why we need Gemmill", Nile said to Ga 'telly.

Ga 'telly didn't bring Gemmill as he knew he needed someone he trusted to stay behind and help everyone else. It dimmed his thoughts even thinking about it.

Ga 'telly shook his head, "I cannot", he said, disappointed, "our computers have tried to contact them for a while, and they have failed".

"But why not boost them up again?" Floyd asked as he walked up to some caught-up wires near the computers. "You never asked anyone to repair them?"

"Stay where you are, Floyd!" Nile told him directly.

"I was only going to help", Floyd suggested.

"It's got nothing to do with us", Ga 'telly explained, "Talen Space places interference into our communications so that we can't reach our allies".

"What kind of interference?" Floyd asked. "Trust me, I'm not going to touch your stuff".

"The power of the cloud".

"Come again?" Floyd asked cluelessly.

"There's something deep within that sector of space", Ga 'telly spoke haunted, "something is powering the Shatter Cloud, something so powerful. We saw it as we barely escaped".

There was a chill within the group as they knew trouble was about to happen very soon. Ga 'telly had the feeling when he spoke - the fear, the terrible, terrible horror that will await them. There was no choice but to stay out for good, but will that be the case?

"Do me a favour," Ga 'telly warned as he was heading back to his bed, "Go back where you came from; this is your only warning".

****

While Floyd, Ryan and Nile headed back down to the shipping dock, a bunch of unpleasant men were in front of the Edwin, as though they were about to do some real bad damage on it.

"Hey!" Nile called as he raced over to them. They turned their heads and faced their visitors. "What do you think you're doing?!"

"You shouldn't come here!" one of the men replied. "You will get yourself killed!"

"Then that's the sort of action we'll take", Nile replied as he eyed the men. They gave Nile an angry stare which warned him to be careful. Nile stared back with an honest look as he headed back into the Edwin.

Floyd and Ryan followed Nile's lead, while Floyd gave out a funny smile to wish them all luck.

8. Entering Territory

They head into Talen Space. It wasn't too far now till the real danger struck. They were now fully aware of their surroundings and wondering whether their mission was a mistake.

Nile wanted to continue piloting since he knew what he was doing. He felt like this was primarily his mission; he grew up in Talen Space and got away years later, so he should return a favour. He also wanted to find out what happened in there; he was young at the time and didn't know even half of the stories there.

Onboard the ship, the Edwin had different rooms. It had a hallway with few quarters that could fit a crew of nine. Floyd and Ryan thought they might kill the time by exploring the ship.

They knew this could be a one-way trip and their chances of survival were getting slimmer by the minute. Floyd tested the calculations while he was in his cell and knew what the right outcome was if they failed.

Floyd was in the bathroom, looking at himself in a mirror pretending his muscles were strong. He was thinking about how buff he was after beating Blok, whom Floyd guessed he would never beat in a hundred years and so on.

"You think you can challenge?" Floyd talked to himself as he pretended to punch. "Were you ready for that? I didn't think so".

As cowardly as this was, Floyd knew he never wanted to make a big fool of himself - even a bigger one. He kept pretending to punch as Ryan walked in. Ryan had no idea what Floyd was doing. Floyd didn't realise that Ryan was watching him until he looked at him.

"Agghh!" Floyd screamed as he jumped, "Wha…what are you doing here?"

"Just checking on you," Ryan said, concerned about his friend. "Were you training?"

"Ye...I mean, no", Floyd refused to answer, "I was…making myself breakfast".

"Breakfast?" Ryan asked, "but it's sixteen passes".

"Oh", Floyd didn't know that. "Then I was doing nothing", he said as he put on his robe.

Yes, even librarians sometimes take off their robes.

As much as Ryan was little help on this trip, he could not stop seeing it was the greatest and the most bizarre of adventures. He liked it. "Is this what you do all the time?"

Floyd replied, "Not really. We mostly ran, ran away and just fixed a few things here and there." Then another thought came to him, "But mostly, yes".

Floyd did jump straight into action because the entire universe was at stake, but he did miss quite the obvious with his friends on the way, "I only met your grandfather the one time".

"Ahh", Ryan replied, "and how did all that go?"

"Pretty terrible, I guess." Floyd thought about it quite often. He wasn't lying; he and Ryan's Grandfather had a rather horrible time. "For him anyway. He always had a thing of not interfering with things you don't understand".

At that moment, Ryan wondered to himself if he was like his grandfather a little bit. Not wanting the crazy adventure he needed, staying away from strange things and never ever seeing them again. Maybe he was like that, but Ryan wanted to change, a change that his grandfather never accepted.

"You know what, Floyd," Ryan said as Floyd turned from the mirror, "you could show me around a bit".

At that moment, Floyd was thrilled, but he didn't know what may happen after their mission.

"Well, we'll just see if we come back alive".

"Yeah," Ryan agreed.

****

The Edwin was already heading into Talen Space not too far away. Floyd and Ryan headed to the piloting room where Nile was. They could barely see any stars; it was all darkness.

Nile was comfortable to set the ship to 'still'.

"Is this it?" Floyd asked Nile from behind.

"We're about forty feet away", Nile replied.

"Why is it so empty?" Ryan asked as he could see nothing. Ryan had a really bad feeling, one that would shake you as if you had a terrible dream.

"Nothing?" Floyd thought about it. Their journey, their most extensive trip with all the trouble they encountered, and they came to nowhere.

Floyd laughed, "Now that's funny; the biggest threat to the human race is basically nothing".

"Quiet down," Ryan told Floyd, fearing that something unknown was staring them in the face. "We don't really know what's out here".

"He is right", Nile agreed, "there's something out here, but we don't know what".

Then, as the Edwin drifted a bit further in, some dark shadow pulled them right in. It was too difficult to notice; it looked like it was part of the blackness of space.

While the ship rocked, Ryan and Floyd tried to hold on to their seats.

"Oh Gosh! oh Gosh!" Ryan repeated even though he hated repeating himself while being totally scared.

"Saying that isn't going to help, Ryan!!!!" Floyd yelled out.

The Edwin stopped and they could see nothing from their windows, but they could hear rattling noises.

"What is that?" Ryan asked as he closed his eyes.

"Ryan, down!" Floyd told him to get under the seat. Ryan listened to his demand.

There was a mystery in this shadow; they had no idea what was controlling it; it felt like it was alive and wanted them.

"What are we facing here, Officer Nile!" Floyd demanded as though he thought he was assisting.

"It looks like we're stuck", Nile pointed out as he tried to flick some of his switches which did nothing.

"Well, that's a good thing", Floyd thought; surely.

"No, it isn't! if we're stuck out here, there will be no way of getting anywhere".

"What if you try to start up your engine to full and brush right through it?" Ryan suggested while staying under his seat.

"Ryan, what have I said while we're in a massive crisis here?" Floyd said, and then looked at Nile and told him, "What if we should start up the engine to full, and we'll brush through the shadow to see how far it would get us".

"I was going to agree with Ryan's plan, anyway," Nile thought.

"Then it will work!" Floyd thought.

Nile clicked on the engine to full, but he knew they weren't travelling at tremendous speed; they travelled slowly, and they all wondered why.

Its tank was full so it could max out its speed and push through the shadow's control.

The Edwin pushed through as the shadow tried to block it. Nile tried to use more power, but the Edwin travelled slowly.

As much as they tried to get through, the shadow eventually took control and dragged the ship.

"We must not follow where it wants to take us!!" Nile called out.

"WHY?!?!?!" Ryan cried out.

"That's where the Shatter Cloud is and their Master!"

"Do you think their master wants to play a game of Sa Rays?" Floyd asked Nile.

"No, they want control! They don't want anything to do with us!"

Nile tried to put the ship in shape as hard as it could. He wanted to shake off the shadow, but it was holding them too firm, and Nile's face was dripping with sweat.

"I can't shake it!"

"Then don't let it take us!" Floyd told Nile, hoping that wouldn't be the case. "Whatever is taking us, it is be better to go where the rest of them were headed".

Despite the situation they were in, Nile was too tired to do anything; he had no control.

"But I can't control it!"

"You must!" Floyd told him that they had no other choice.

Nile didn't want to; he thought it would make it angrier and crash their ship. He closed his eyes and took a deep breath. He could do it; he had to believe. No matter how impossible, there was no winning if he lost control.

Nile tried to break off the shadow's control. He was trying to lift the ship out of the shadow, even taking different approaches and ways of breaking it off. Then Nile had an idea that might break it; if he could decode the speed as fast as anything, it might break the shadow's control. He touched the buttons and pushed the console as powerfully as he could.

Floyd noticed the shadow's strength as it was scrapping the Edwin. This wasn't a good sign; it made Floyd freak.

But then the shadow was breaking off as if something was harming it. It was fading in a way, and it was continuing to fade till it was way off.

The Edwin burst out of it as it sped towards a nearby planet; it was smoky and looked very polluted.

"We got out of it," Nile said in relief.

Floyd looked down at Ryan and told him, "Get up; it's over".

Ryan looked up as it was gone, relieved that nothing so bad happened to them.

"That was bizarre" he commented.

As hard as it was, Nile was struggling the most. He had not felt much pressure from an escape that lost him his job; but now, he was just glad it was over, for the moment.

"It must have been the black cloud where they take the humans." Nile speculated.

"Wherever it was taking them, it's where we'll find them," said Floyd knowing that this could be the place to find every answer.

"If we were following it. Should we not be following it?" Ryan asked, thinking very logically.

Oh, Great, he was thinking more like his grandfather, Floyd, thought. But Floyd's face was curious about the question; he had that thought for a long time, then simply said "I just go with it".

Ryan looked out the window, where he saw the planet below them. He could see what the world looked like. It was foggy, and he felt like no one would like this world. "Where are we?" Ryan asked Nile.

"The human's last home world," Nile explained.

Floyd looked at him and said, "And how do you know that?"

"Because I was raised here".

9. The Last Human Colony

The Edwin came downwards to the planet to take a closer look. They flew through the big dark grey clouds in front of the windows and could hardly see what was beyond that.

Floyd ate pieces of candy out of his hands, picking them out piece by piece. He later offered them to Ryan, "Want some?"

"When did you get them?" Ryan asked as he couldn't imagine what sort of time Floyd had to get treats.

"Nile gave them to me when I was still held in the cell; it was only to get me to be quiet".

"And it did the little job, didn't it?" Nile said, as he knew no other tricks would've stopped Floyd from his ongoing stories.

Ryan looked out of the window with his feet on the seat; besides being a safety caution, it was more comfortable. "I can't see anything".

"You'll see it soon enough," said Nile as they flew out of the cloud.

They saw a city with a massive population. There were buildings shaped like cubes in every street; they were built on top of each other so that it looked like they were made of building blocks stacked like a tower. They could hear the noises of vehicles and hundreds of people below. There would be a million of them out here. The last human colony.

This was a planet of mayhem. A planet to cause chaos. How could anyone live here? And why?

Nile had some details about this planet; it felt like it was home to him, and indeed it was. The lost son had returned home.

"This wasn't a nice place," Nile explained as he remembered the old times. "Everyone had to find a place to stay, but it was too crowded".

"Then why are there too many?" Floyd asked, giving close attention to the city below.

"Because this is the reason, Floyd", Nile said as he looked at the librarian, "there is too much stuff for the human race".

Floyd couldn't understand any of this; his head wouldn't accept it. There must be something trying to kill them off, or worse, feed off them.

"But either way, they were brought here with little choice", Nile commented, "the Shatter Cloud brought them here to serve whatever it is".

"The Shadow?" Ryan asked.

"Must be".

"But I know what will happen; but none of this is meant to happen", said Floyd knowing every fact of history in his brain.

"How would you know?" Ryan asked about a billion times.

Floyd gave him a worried look as he tried not to talk; he had a shaky smile and then went back to his objective. "As this is the place that was killing them off, what is killing them?" Floyd wondered.

Before Nile could reply, Ryan interrupted, "Let's go down and have a look".

Floyd and Nile turn and looked at Ryan.

"You want to go and have a look?" Floyd asked

Ryan. "You really want to take a look down at the dangerous, hopeless, and…".

"Don't worry, kid", Nile replied to get Floyd off his back, "I'll take us down".

Floyd looked surprised; he wasn't too sure if anyone was going to listen to him again.

****

As they landed, they saw the big, polluted buildings more clearly; they were smoky and packed together. Everything seemed so busy here, but funny enough, there were only a few people around in the immediate area. It must have been a tranquil place.

Floyd, Nile and Ryan walked through the street as people wondered about. Everything seemed off right from the start. It wasn't so busy, and everyone tried to move less in crowds.

It made Floyd and his pals suspicious that something would happen, but nothing alerted them.

"Why do you think everyone seems to be acting…weird?". Ryan asked his friends.

"Because they're trying not to draw any attention", Nile replied.

"Why not?" Floyd asked.

"Because it would only alert the Shatter Cloud," Nile told them as he tried to look around the street they were on, "they take anyone to the other side".

"Other side?" Ryan asked.

"To a different planet", Nile continued, "that's where their master is".

"Sounds a bit creepy if you ask me," Floyd thought, "I'm surprised that these guys would want to do that sort of thing. Serving an evil entity".

"That's what you think this is?" Ryan asked Floyd, "an alien life form?"

"No, something stronger than that", Floyd thought, "I think it hungers for power. Maybe it's using the members of the Shatter Clouds as Pawns so it would grow more stronger, so it would conquer the galaxy".

Nile looked with startling eyes, showing how that worried him, "I don't like what you're saying, Floyd. If that is what you think it is doing, we cannot waste any more time".

"My point exactly," Floyd thought as Ryan tapped him on the shoulder. As they saw some kind of trembling vehicle coming toward to them. It had blue tiles and about eight tires, and it looked threatening.

Ryan and Nile asked Floyd if he could give them an order or a way to do something about the vehicle; Floyd looked blank.

"Well, don't look at me," said Floyd as he didn't have any better plan, "run!"

They ran from the Tumbler; the Tumbler was quite large, and the wheels quickly caught up. It had a determination to keep up as Floyd realized running wouldn't do anything; it would only weaken them.

While they kept running as if it posed no problem, another vehicle arrived in front of them. It was an average earth truck staring right in front of them. Floyd thought it would've killed them if it didn't stop so neatly.

"The Revolutionary!" Nile called remembering the alliance against the Shatter Cloud.

Floyd and the others stopped running, and then people jumped out of the truck and tried to grab Floyd and his friends into the truck.

"Get inside!" said one of the rescuers. He looked like he wore a chest plate. Then as Floyd, Ryan, and Nile settled in, the truck drove off and the Tumbler followed them into the street.

10. The Truck Street Chase

The truck that Floyd, Ryan, and Nile were in drove right into another street. The street was tight with people all around; the drivers were hoping not to hit any of them as people quickly noted them and got out of the way.

The truck was filled with Revolutionary members; they wore unclean clothes, and their faces were dirty like they had dust on them not long ago. Few of them had bulletproof shirts, weapons, riffles, and blasters.

But not too far behind, the Shatter Cloud's Tumbler was gaining on them; they weren't going to leave them till they were captured. The Tumbler had sharp windows on each side, like a giant bullet with amour and shielding.

They drove through streets in every direction; they took different paths, and each path always had an end. Thankfully not one of them got hurt.

"Don't hit anyone!!" yelled Floyd to the driver.

"Alright, mum!" said the driver.

Floyd wasn't sure if these guys were well trained or just causing havoc as though everywhere said, "Hit Me! Hit Me!"

The Tumbler was gaining closer to them; it wouldn't be long till they had a tremendous advantage for hitting them. They were only a few meters apart from each other. A few Revolutionaries took out their weapons and fired at the Tumbler. It had minor effects because the Tumbler's steel was unable to be harmed by their blast.

"Why didn't it work?!" yelled Ryan, trying to get attention and not be left out.

No one was going to answer him as some were firing on the Tumbler, but some just didn't want to talk, except one, "Because none of our weapons work on it!"

"Then why are you firing?!" Floyd asked him, standing up.

"Because we need to drive them back!" said the trooper, "we need time to lose it!"

"That's so stupid!" Ryan called out.

"No! I've seen stupid!" said Nile, trying to be encouraging, while Floyd wasn't so impressed.

The truck took a heavy and hard turn, making everyone on board fall over. The truck tried to increase speed while the Tumbler moved closer to them.

The Tumbler crew were thinking of clamouring in more closely as they bumped and crashed into the truck, making everyone fall over again.

"Can we lose this as a habit, please!" said Floyd annoyed.

The firing kept going, with no effect, damage, or harm; the Tumbler was still in one piece. While the chase and the firing were going on, poor Ryan was lying on the floor, trying to process these crazy events around him. Were these bad guys? Properly? Maybe they forgot to get their big, fried chicken burger that the other guys didn't want to get refunded.

While Ryan was watching the battle unfold, he knew in his mind that he wanted to help out. He spotted something under a blanket; he wasn't sure what, but he took it out. What was this big object that looked like it could fire a dozen mountains? Wait, Mountains! If Ryan could time and aim it perfectly…

He pulled the switch, and a big, loud fire beamed into the Tumbler forcing it to back away, and roll backwards, catching itself on fire. The Revolutionary team cheered.

Ryan was still holding onto the mighty weapon as he wasn't sure what to do with it; Ryan was no expert on any weaponry, nor was his grandfather Jack.

Ryan stood up and tried to get a clear shot with nothing interfering with him. "I got it!" Ryan called out.

Then Floyd looked at him, "Ryan, put that down! It's not a toy!"

"I got it, Floyd!" recalled Ryan, taking an excellent clear shot; he could shoot it down.

They were waiting for the perfect moment; after these hard turns and big thumps and all the other stuff, this was the moment Ryan couldn't miss.

Ryan shot again, and the Tumbler exploded while chasing on fire and rolling down the street. Ryan could almost have fallen backwards, but he stood still.

The attack was impressive; it took care of the Tumbler, it seriously took care of it, but everyone knew that this was not a success for taking down a whole army.

✱✱✱✱✱✱✱✱✱✱✱✱✱✱✱✱✱✱✱✱✱✱✱✱✱✱✱✱✱✱

Not long afterward, the Revolutionary celebrated their recent successful attack, and Ryan was especially rewarded for helping; he was given a bunch of 2000s Earth cash that would mean nothing in this decade. He kept it in his pocket for the road; it might still be worth a fortune. He was buffed out of air. Floyd was sitting next to him.

As much as Floyd had mixed reactions about Ryan's rash actions, he knew more about Ryan than Nile with weapons. For Ryan's effort, he assured him, "You did excellent!"

Ryan was still tired and without breath, but he said with one last breath, "Thanks".

"No, I mean, you were awesome!" Floyd kept saying. "You took a good clear shot, then BOOM! You took out the Tumbler".

It was like his brain was blown up over and over again, while he wanted to get some tickets to a lovely planet.

Nile walked past and gave Ryan a generous smile, "You did great," he said truthfully.

He had some talk with the other Revolutionary members; he heard that they were going to meet Gemmill. They mentioned that they were on their way to her at this very moment.

Ryan and Floyd weren't sure what was going on with him, but they knew that he was making progress.

"You know what might happen to Nile?" Ryan asked, as they hadn't talked about him much on their journey.

"Who knows, maybe he might stay and help. Down through the years, he always needed to know what was going on in the cosmos and try to do things right".

"Like putting you in a cell for trespassing?" Ryan thought jokingly.

"Yeah, stuff like that." Floyd wasn't sure what might happen to him, but he took a lucky guess. "Don't worry about that, Ryan; just, for now, think about how amazing you were".

"Yeah," Ryan said, as he had never faced anything like it, "I was, wasn't I?"

"Yeah," Floyd responded, "you knew what you were doing while I was just sitting in the back row, chatting about".

Then Floyd realised how much fun that was again, like back in those times, facing scary scenarios with great people helping beside him. Maybe…maybe Ryan was a good discovery after all.

Then somebody in the driving seat called, "We have incoming! We're almost there!"

They hid inside a tunnel. On the other side, two more Tumblers drove by, missing them. They checked around the area to see if they could escort any humans. It took them about five minutes to leave the tunnel and head to Gemmill.

11. Blending in to not be a Fool

It took a few minutes till they reached their destination; it was already dark and quiet, and nobody was around on the street where they were.

The truck drove through a light tunnel. The tunnel was glowing with bright orange light all the way. It was quite a pretty sight just for this moment.

Then when they arrived at the base, it was full of trucks and men carrying cargo. Boxes were everywhere, like many bases have. They could see the dark sky above. It had a shivering feeling that Ryan couldn't shake; he could tell whatever was out there was lurking.

In front of them was a building. The only facility in the area. The whole place was blocked by tall walls. It felt like a ruin from the Greek islands.

The person in the driver seat got out and walked up to Floyd and his friends.

"Thank you!" Floyd said as a check-up crew checked all over Floyd and his friends, "Easy Now!"

"Gemmill will be waiting for you," the driver said as he walked into the base.

Floyd turned his head to his pals; how did she know?

The guy started to grab Floyd's arm to go with him, "OK! OK!" Floyd said to the guy, "not too hasty". Ryan and Nile tagged along with them as they entered the base.

****

It was like one of those Greek stone tunnels; the floor was smooth like an old army base, with the same orange light above them throughout the place. The place felt very tight as they hoped they wouldn't have to squeeze into areas that wouldn't fit five people.

They walked through tunnels that curled like a snake. Revolutionary members were walking by, and a few were sitting on comfortable chairs with lanterns. It seemed like everyone was quite at home; this was just the place Ryan would like if he could hardly see.

"I see everyone is nicely at home, right?" Floyd asked, while he was still grabbed all the way. Ryan and Nile were enjoying seeing him being dragged away while trying not to laugh. "I don't think they chose any other better place to stay low".

"What makes you think that?" Ryan asked, as he and Nile tried to catch up while not bumping into anything.

This was the kind of place you could easily get lost and never find where you came from. It was some complex maze that would shadow you, and then one day, you may remember what the outdoor world was like.

"Because this place seems homey", Floyd added as they entered a room that led up stairs. The door they opened was a steel handled door.

As they arrived up the stairs, they saw a woman standing in the centre with one of those World War planning tables. They could also see the stone tunnels around the place, showing how you could cheat yourself in a maze.

The woman looked tired; she had dark skin with long black hair that was tied up and wore a clean white shirt.

"You could have blown your cover," she said in a lower voice; she wasn't looking at them, focusing on the table that had the map of the whole planet. It felt like she was the master planner that wanted to see events play out without being a part of them.

"Well, it wasn't my idea to blow my cover; just letting you know," said Floyd, trying to be reasonable.

The woman looked up like she doesn't care, "Are you daft?" she asked as she walked up to Floyd, "They know where you are or where you will be. You think these guys don't care if they saw something coming out of the sky and landing on this junkyard!"

"Well, if you ask me," began Floyd, as Gemmill was right at his face. Floyd felt terminated; it felt like termination. "I have known a few Junkyards in my history, and this isn't in the top one hundred".

While their conversion went on, a man played with the communication equipment and tried to send signals. "Beep, Boob, Beep!" he said like he was speaking sound effects.

"Is he making sound effects?" Ryan asked Nile.

"Yes, he makes technology sound effects to keep himself focused".

"Well, isn't it a bit...".

"What?".

"...a bit odd?"

"Well, they don't seem to mind. I don't see why we're bothering him".

Gemmill had enough of fools. Fools that had plans to get themselves killed or caught. She stood up and sighed heavily. "OK, what's your deal?" she asked as she wanted to get to the catch.

"Thank you for asking," Floyd said as he also wanted to move to that catch as well, "we wanted to help".

"Wait, you?" Gemmill said, as if she could burst into laughter, "You came all the way out here to help while wearing that dress?"

"Hey!" called Ryan, "we came this far, and we've been through so much. The least you can do is give us a bit of slack!"

Gemmill watched them and sighed, "Yeah, you're right," she said briefly, "maybe I've been doing this for too long". She glared at them once again, "You really want to go through with this? Where you will be going might cost you more lives than you have".

"That's why we're here," replied Nile, who was the only person who stood out in the room. "We need to take whatever is out there down; no more fear; it ends today".

"Yeah," said Floyd agreeing, "like, what he said".

Gemmill really liked their tones; maybe they had a bit of something she hadn't seen in them before, and that might be the hope humanity needed right now.

Gemmill smiled like she hadn't had a good joke for a long time and looked at Nile, "You've been in this region of space, haven't you?".

Nile's face showed he had seen everything he needed to know. Then Gemmill walked back and said, "If you want to head where the Shatter Cloud have taken the people, you need to blend in; we have some of their uniforms here".

Then with that, Ryan thought, "We can do that" there wasn't a corner of his mind that this would fail.

"Hey Floyd," said Nile next to him, as he tried to make Floyd relax, "how do you feel about being our prisoner?"

$$*****************************$$

As the next sun rose, Ryan and Nile took Floyd to one of the nearest transports to take them where the Shatter Cloud had been taking the missing humans.

Ryan and Nile wore sleek black and grey plates and helmets covering their faces up to their noses. The helmets were like a mask; a bit more like imposing skulls that shone in the darkness into anyone's soul.

Floyd wore futuristic hand covers that were hard for him to get out of. "This is so silly!" Floyd complained, not liking the idea.

They stopped at a large metal door; they had a code to bypass. That was one thing they didn't know about, "How are we meant to get in?" Ryan asked as they had no clue what to do from here.

"Just use that helmet of yours…" said Floyd while being interrupted.

"We get the idea," said Nile as he kneeled forwards for the machine to scan the helmet.

The machine was trying to figure out who he was, then some good ding sound appeared, and the door opened sideways. How they got in must be some code inside the helmet that their friends had hacked the passcode.

"See?" Nile told Floyd. "It wasn't so hard, was it?"

When they walked inside, it was an outdoor outpost transporting area. Many guards were wandering the area and transporting prisoners to the ships that were lined up.

There were many ships in the area, five at least, each as big as an ordinary house. They had silk sides with scales like dragonflies on their corners, and white with a blue stripe on either side.

"Can we get to one?" Floyd tried to get his two-prison guards' attention.

"Yeah, we better," Nile agreed, "these ships will be taking off in less than five minutes, and we had better not get recognised by anyone here".

"Good idea", Ryan replied, "then, we better take Floyd with us?"

"We better," said Nile.

"We better?" Floyd asked behind them, as they thought it would be a terrible idea to give him to another stranger.

Then they walked up to the nearest ship whose floor hatch was open, and a bunch of soldiers headed inside.

When Floyd, Ryan and Nile were inside the ship, it took off effortlessly. As they entered out of orbit, there was no trouble but a few heavy shakes of the ship. And the ship was heading to its mysterious destination.

12. The Place of the Forgotten

It took several hours to reach the planet. They only could hear the rattling of the ship; this could bring someone's attention to it as if there was something wrong with the ship. But it was always meant to be like this when they were about to reach the planet.

The prisoners were in an area with bars. They also saw how many soldiers were all over the place. The soldiers weren't doing much; they just sat there while the prisoners did the same.

The light was glim as it was pretty dark in there, and there weren't any windows, so it was hard to tell the time or location. The only thing they heard about the planet was, it was so dark that you could barely see it.

It wasn't the most cosy trip if you were not listening to Floyd's long tales. The soldiers wondered what he was on about.

Floyd was chattering to the prisoner next to him;

something about how Milk would turn into a wave and cause a high expansion of science. He was also busy watching what the soldiers were doing. "What are they waiting for?" he asked himself.

"They are waiting for the arrival," said the prisoner on the other side, who was near the door of the cell.

Floyd turned and studied him. He was like the people on the street: daggy, unshaven and looking like a guy you don't think you could trust. "And you are?"

"Gammon", the man replied.

"How would you know we are arriving?" Floyd asked as he hasn't had this ride before.

The guy gave Floyd a weird gesture that looked like he may have no clue, "Lucky guess".

For some reason, if they were going to be somewhere as bad as this, Floyd thought he may as well make a new friend. "I can tell you've got friends on board" Gammon said.

"I do…".

"Your lying," Gammon said. He knew Floyd was going to say it was the person next to him. He knew what kind of a person someone like Floyd would make friends with: the well informed who knew stuff that others didn't. What other people may not know about Gammon was that he read people by the look on their faces.

"You know I've seen people lying because they have a plan", Gammon explained.

"No, I don't" Floyd replied as Gammon stood up and grabbed Floyd by the shirt. Gammon winked a smile, as if their plans would work somehow.

A guard tapped on the bar indicating he wanted them to be quiet. Floyd sat down with the others and took the quiet ride to this new world. But who was this Gammon? Why was he so helpful?

****

It wasn't too long before the ship landed. The Shatter Cloud finally took the prisoners out into the bright light and what they saw of the place was incredible. It was like normal daylight, but with mountains of ruins. It wasn't exactly pretty; it was like a mining world that would have been destroyed a hundred years ago.

Where they were going was a nearby cave that went right inside the nearest mountain. The tunnel was quite big, and with it was a mining camp where there were other humans and their Guards to keep an eye on them.

Floyd had no exact words to describe all of this, but this must be what they were doing to all the rest of the humans. They were using humans as tools to do the dirty work for the Shatter Cloud, or was it a way for execution?

This wasn't meant to be a prison or a trap; this was the key to the death of humanity. Floyd puzzled everything together and didn't like the odds.

Not that long after, both Ryan and Nile stopped Floyd in his tracks, and quickly hid in one of the nearest ships.

They took off Floyd's handcuff, and Nile and Ryan took off their helmets before furthering their plan.

"OK," said Nile, "you two try to blend in and find a way to alert the prisoners while I try to break free the force field and send the Revolutionary our location".

"Hey, who made you in charge of stuff?" Floyd said in sarcasm, "anyway, I met this guy…".

"Who?" Ryan asks.

"Never mind", Floyd continued, "but I have a very, very, very, very deep thought he could help out".

Nile gave him the stare that said Floyd never surprised him, "You're going to get him, aren't you?"

"I know we all have a lot at stake right now, but if I could try to get him, he could really be helpful".

Nile wanted to debate Floyd in these matters, but other matters were at stake. "I want you to get all that done as soon as possible".

"That will hardly be a problem," said Ryan, agreeing with the plan, "right Floyd?"

Floyd was in a thinking state; he was calculating their successes. When his journey began, it was about 60%, but after learning about the whole extinction of humanity thing, it came to around 30%, then The Shatter Cloud involvement, 13%. By now, it was still 13%.

Nile grunted, "We don't have time for this! We have to shut it now, or it will be over!"

Nile put his helmet back on and left them be. Floyd wondered if there would be any chance for their plan to work at all.

****

Floyd and Ryan saw a whole load of people digging up some rich diamonds and stuff inside the mining cave. This could have been some material the Shatter Cloud needed, needed for technology that there was no way anyone in the universe could get a hold of.

"This material is so dense!" Ryan said. "How could they ever find something like this?"

"I have no idea", Floyd thought, "so we have to move swiftly".

The two later walked over a bridge through the wide cave, which went a long way. Ryan and Floyd just kept casual as they moved further in.

They noticed how big the place was; they couldn't imagine a world that was so massive and wide and expansive like this that also seemed so far off. Floyd couldn't shake that, though.

But it caught their surprise when someone hopped in their way. It was Gammon!

It caught Floyd off guard and almost to his soul. "What are you doing here?"

"I slipped pass one of the prison guards, it wasn't easy," he replied, "but don't worry, none of them noticed me. They are incredibly stupid". He joined them, and they knelt down while watching the other prisoners being held, "What's the plan?"

"Plan One does not involve any killing. Plan Two is to lure them into a spooky tunnel to trap them in" Floyd turned to Gammon and asked him, "Is there a spooky tunnel we can trap them in?"

"I think so", Gammon replied.

"Good enough…" Floyd said.

Just then, a watch guard came over to them, suspicious. Floyd and Ryan knew they would be caught, but they weren't expecting to be caught this early.

They try not to panic, especially Floyd. His expression was all over the place, trying not to eyeball the guard.

"What's your distinct number?" asked the guard to Ryan.

"Distinct number?" Ryan asked, "Nahhhh…".

"It's, um…" Floyd tried to reply as if he was taking Ryan's spot; Floyd clearly said he was taking over.

"05784265319272-AD4457221UIS-something to do with your favourite Cat…".

"Imposters!!!" said the guard as he wielded out a small gun. Before it fired, Gammon tackled the guard onto the ground while Ryan rushed over to the nearest hill where he could get the prisoner's attention.

"Listen to me!" Ryan said with his helmet off, "I have come here to set you all free! We may not be the civilisation as we used to be, but we cannot be dominated by these beasts! I want to take you all to a new stage of humanity!"

"Go at 'em, Kid!" Floyd cheered him on as Gammon kept beating off the guard.

Ryan looked at the curious faces of the prisoners looking around him, wondering who this kid was?

"I know it's dull and weird, and you may be thinking "Who's this guy doing a Great speech that looks like he came from a Movie", but the thing is we have to act immediately!"

At that moment, there were meant to be people cheering him, but what he got was confused people and guards pointing their guns at his head.

Ryan wasn't too sure what he might add next, "And I'll give you all a raise!"

Then everyone cheered. They fought back as they knocked down the guards and took their weapons. Soon they were fighting back and kicking the guards, and a lot of them ran away. All over the place the two sides fought, and one was fighting for survival.

Ryan walked down to Floyd who cheered him all the way. "That was excellent!" Floyd said, "the thing with the raise and everything!"

At that moment, they heard a big blast upwards, and they could see through the big hole of the cave were the ships of the Revolutionary. But there was more than they expected: Ga'Telly! So, he did come, after all!

"Oh boy! They're here!" Floyd called out, "we have to head out!"

****

When they got outside, the Revolutionary's ships were docking as prisoners were running to them. The Revolutionaries were fighting inward and trying to take the entire base.

The Shatter Cloud were falling behind as most of them planned to leave the planet. The Revolutionaries kept on fighting as they were drawing near to winning with the help of the prisoners.

The Shatter Cloud didn't stand a chance, with such a mighty force as this, they planned to leave the planet and never return. As their ships took off in the air, the Revolutionaries' ships shot them down so they couldn't escape.

Nile was at one of the nearest ships where he was fighting as well, and this was a fight he had been waiting for, for a very long time.

He spotted Floyd and Ryan running towards him with other prisoners. "Floyd! Ryan!" he called out, "you got here safe".

"Are we good?" Ryan asked, "we got everyone, and it sounds like we might be winning?"

"Yes, Ryan, I think we have", Nile responded, "but I do have some bad news".

"Bad news?!" Floyd hesitated, "how could THIS be bad news?" Their luck had been much beyond what they imagined; there couldn't be anything much worse if they were winning.

Nile handed them a tablet of some kind. "As you recall, we keep getting stuck in the side of Talen Space; there is an energy reading around here, and I've heard something is going to go down".

"Go down?" Floyd asks, "like what?"

Nile's expression wasn't telling much, "I don't know, but we better get off this rock for good".

They ran towards the Edwin, but in the front was Gammon; he was waiting for them. For some reason, he waved to them, "I was waiting…".

"NO TIME!" Floyd told him as they entered. The one thing Gammon didn't tell them was that he had five other prisoners to hitch the ride as well. That was something Nile was going to talk about later.

As they left off, the rest of the Revolutionary left as well, as they knew something bad was happening. But what they all didn't realize was the change in the sky.

13. Darker than Clouds

As the ships took off, they noticed that the clouds were getting darker, with a purplier colour.

Ryan, Nile, Floyd, and newcomer Gammon had no clue what was going on, but the sky was different.

"Hey, what's going on?" Ryan asked.

"The colour looks different," Gammon said very idiotically.

Nile turned on the lights, but as the lights tried to turn on, nothing had any effect.

"Now that's strange," he said strangely.

The cloud was dark and grizzly. Like there was nothing that could prepare you for what was on the other side. It stuck with bloomy air and gas of chill.

No one could tell what they were seeing, or how the cloud could change so immediately. Something was buzzing their minds and they couldn't tell what it was.

The next thing that happened was strange; the

cloud itself roared and made itself into a dragon-like form but still part of the cloud.

Everyone jumped and screamed; it was coming at them with its mouth open; the Edwin was the size of an insect next to it.

Nile planned to back up the Edwin away from it. "Down! Down! Down!" Nile panicked. The Edwin moved away from the dragon as the dragon faded into the cloud, out of sight.

"What was that!!!" Floyd said in a high tone.

"The storm", Nile told him, "hold on!!!" He pushed the lever as the ship drove further into the cloud. The whole sky was full of it, and they didn't know what they might hit. It was rather difficult to identify what, exactly.

Shortly after, a dragon's tail smacked the Edwin as it sprung. Everyone knocked into one side of the ship with that heavy hit.

"It didn't damage the ship, but it'll try next time!" Nile said, giving out the warning.

On the other side, they could see the Revolutionary ships also fighting back; they flew upwards and tried to escape but exploded in the process. The cloud hit a few of the vessels as they exploded.

It was difficult to determine what part of the cloud the creature was. But the hard thing was that this entire cloud was part of it. It was as if a single entity had become the cloud with incredible power! As the ships flowed and fired, they had great difficulty escaping.

The passengers on the Edwin were having a hard time figuring out what was going on, while Nile tried to get them to calm down and put seat belts on.

Nile pushed the ship up in the sky again at full speed. He noticed that other ships were doing the same too, hoping that they would get out smoothly and safely.

He later saw some other tails trying to wrack them. He dodged with mighty spins. It made Ryan quite impressed; it made Floyd quizzy, and it made the others quite sick.

"That was radical!!" said Gammon, who was the only one enjoying himself.

"Not Now!!!" Floyd told him.

But that was the least of their troubles. The dragon's face rose near to them as it roared at the nearest ships.

"Gotta get out of here!" Nile screamed as the Edwin made its getaway.

The dragon's head tilted forward as some other ships exploded. Later, while the Edwin was still playing cat and mouse, the shadow of the dragon lay underneath them and then next to them.

Nile did his best to avoid the dragon's tails, but he knew that this creature wasn't going to leave them.

The ship did quite well not getting destroyed, but as one tail struck, one of the engines got hit, and the ship dived down. It flew down while clouds separated; it was only about sixteen thousand feet or less till it crashed to the surface.

"Oh, crud!" said Nile as something hit his stomach and bounced off, "one of the engines just got hit! We need somebody to repair it immediately!"

"What!! Who?!" Floyd asked, as he didn't want to do it.

"You should go, Floyd", Ryan suggested.

"Me?!!"

"Yes! You have to try to use the Fixing Computer, but it is extremally dangerous".

"But, why me?"

"That's okay, man," Gammon told him, "I could always go with you".

Ryan tried to think of some excuse that would make Floyd more comfortable, but at this stage, nothing was going to be nice.

"So, we can rely on you?"

"Oh, great," Floyd thought, as if that was bad enough. Floyd took the Fixing Computer on his way and opened the engine door hanging outside. "Oh great" he said again, but this time in horror.

He saw that there was a small bridge leading to the engine that was about a foot away; it wasn't easy to fix it while hovering in the air. He saw a sparkle in it as there was much fixing.

The Fixing Computer was a seventieth-century gadget that lined the spanner in the right direction and became fully active.

Floyd looked back at the outside of the engine with fear and worry dripping down from his thoughts.

"Oh great" he said when he put his leg on the closest pillar to the machine. "They could have thought of someone else, but they voted me".

Then not so long after, Ryan came over to him for assistance. "Need a hand?"

"About fifteen seconds ago" Floyd complained, worrying about not being sucked up or mostly sucked down by this planet. This was not the planet he was hoping to see, this wasn't beautiful, this was horrible!!!

"Well, you better get it done in two minutes".

"Well, thanks", Floyd replied, "thanks for the pep talk".

While Floyd was fixing the machine, he could see the thing turning into a dragon's head that was a hundred times bigger than the ship.

"Oh god!" he said shaking, it's over he thought.

Ryan wanted to calm him down, even though he also knew that it was over. All those years of staying alive, all those good times to come, all were now gone. But he never expected to be here in the first place.

He started to calm Floyd down, "Okay, think about something cool".

"How can I think of something cool at a time like this?!" Floyd told Ryan when he got onto the other side of the engine. He took out his tool and it did its work. The spanner glowed lime green around the sparkles.

Ryan knew he had to do better; he thought he might say something better. "Try thinking about how far we came! You arm wrestled a guy into helping us!"

"Yeah, I did" Floyd remembered the match like it was his greatest achievement. It wasn't doing much; the dragon was looking more impressive to them than ever.

"And that accident we had! That was like one in a million chances we could've survived but we did!!"

"Yeah," Floyd said, wondering what was taking the engine so long to be back up online? Before Floyd could continue on his fast-paced work, he looked back at the dragon and saw its mouth winding up.

"Ooooohhh…." Floyd spoke as the dragon closed its mouth.

****

The next stuff was weird. It was dark; no one could see a thing. They were inside the cloud. No buttons, no light, no sound, nothing. There was only an absence of darkness, and nothing happened in those many, many, many minutes.

Was this the end? Just a big journey to reach a certain destination and what? Get eaten up by a clouded dragon?

Is this really how it ends? And we got, what, nine more books in the series and this is how it all ends up? Oh no, we're not having that, Floyd thought.

The creature was in his full stature as the whole fleet had departed and maybe was gone. It was alone and at peace. As it may think, it didn't destroy all the humans, but at least it destroyed as much as it could.

Light flashed onto its face, and it reacted as it tried to close its eyes and move its head away. More light shined as the dark cloud later became bright. A bunch of Revolutionary ships came and acted against it so it would be defeated. All were hoping that the Edwin crew would get out of this alive.

But what happened instead was that the entity itself faded away, and what was left of it was the Edwin.

Nile and the others were relieved that they would not get trapped inside darkness forever. That would be the worst entire lifespan ever.

As the ships took off into the stars, the planet destroyed itself as it had no longer any purpose or any rulers. It was all cast by the Great Beast, and now the Great Beast was gone, humanity was freed!!

The next mission now was to bring the humans back to the Revolutionary base and get everyone off the planet, and then take off to the stars, break out the news and tell them that humanity was not leaving from the stars.

While they made their way back to the Revolutionary base, Floyd and Ryan looked into the window at the piloting room where Nile was taking command.

They could see the stars were freshly clean, with no darkness or anything hiding from them, no evil loaming or scary things. It was fresh and new, stars shined and scattered as there were so many things to discover.

"The darkness is clean, and now, there are even more stars we never imagined before" said Nile noting the wonders of the universe.

Ryan looked over to Floyd who was looking at the stars too, thinking it was no different from before.

Ryan asked, "What will you do now? Are you going to head back to your library?"

Floyd took a deep breath and smelt the deepness of space. "I finally decided there is more to do than just being a librarian".

Ryan looked at him blankly, "So does that mean no?"

"Well, if you put it that way, I might return there. One day" he said, as if he was lying to himself. A librarian always has to return to his post.

He looked at Ryan and asked, "If you don't mind can we stay in touch?"

Ryan looked back at Floyd and replied, "I don't think it's that big of a deal".

"Oh great", Floyd replied and was relieved.
"Well, at least everything worked well in the end".

THE END

www.ingramcontent.com/pod-product-compliance
Lightning Source LLC
Chambersburg PA
CBHW061105100726
47911CB00012B/399